Do plants eat food?

T0364523

Written by Sally Morgan

Illustrated by Ángeles Peinador

Collins

What's in this book?

Listen and say 🎧①

sun

tree

plant

roots

grass

flower

fruit

leaf

sunflower

One day, Jack and Mummy had a picnic.

"Look at the bird!" said Mummy. "It's eating fruit from the tree!"

"So, we eat sandwiches, the bird eats fruit from a plant, but what do plants eat?" asked Jack.

We eat lots of different food. We need food to grow. What food do you eat? What is your favourite food?

Animals eat food, too. This horse is eating grass.

Plants are different. They don't eat food. They make food in their leaves.

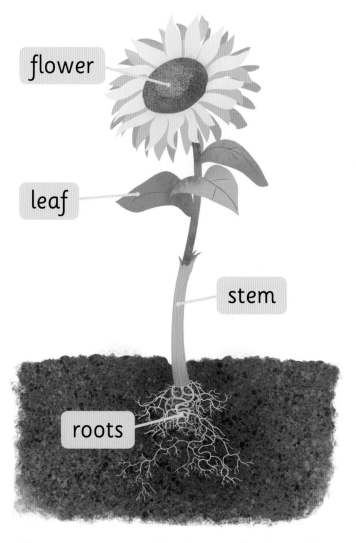

flower

leaf

stem

roots

The sunflower is a tall plant. It has leaves, a stem, a flower and roots.

The leaves grow out of the stem. The roots are in the ground.

seeds

The sunflower makes seeds. Birds eat the seeds.

Some seeds drop on the ground.

Leaves have different shapes. How many shapes can you see?

Some leaves are made from lots of smaller leaves.

Most leaves are green, but some leaves are red and green.

Where can you see red leaves?

Plants need the sun. They grow up to the sun because they need its light.

Plants hold their leaves out. The sun falls on their leaves.

Then the plants make food in their leaves.

The food in their leaves is called sugar.
Some of the sugar goes to the roots.

The plant makes more leaves and grows
more roots and then the plant grows taller.

Roots grow down and hold the plant in the ground.

They stop the plant falling down when it is windy!

Roots take water from the ground.
Water moves up the stem. It goes to
the leaves.

flower

stem

glass

red water

Try this!

Put a white flower in a glass of red water.

Wait for one day. Look at the flower again.

The roots take the water. The colour goes up the stem to the flower.

Now the white flower is red.

House plants live in your home. They need a sunny room and water.

Do you have any house plants?

So, plants do not eat food because they make their food. They also need sun, water and good soil.

Picture dictionary

Listen and repeat 🎧③

house plant

light

seed

soil

stem

sugar

sunny

windy

1 Look and match

flower   grass   leaf   plant

tree   roots   seed

2 Listen and say

Collins

Published by Collins
An imprint of HarperCollins*Publishers*
Westerhill Road
Bishopbriggs
Glasgow
G64 2QT

HarperCollins*Publishers*
1st Floor, Watermarque Building
Ringsend Road
Dublin 4
Ireland

William Collins' dream of knowledge for all began with the publication of his first book in 1819.

A self-educated mill worker, he not only enriched millions of lives, but also founded a flourishing publishing house. Today, staying true to this spirit, Collins books are packed with inspiration, innovation and practical expertise. They place you at the centre of a world of possibility and give you exactly what you need to explore it.

© HarperCollins*Publishers* Limited 2020

10 9 8 7 6 5 4 3 2

ISBN 978-0-00-839680-0

Collins® and COBUILD® are registered trademarks of HarperCollins*Publishers* Limited

www.collins.co.uk/elt

British Library Cataloguing in Publication Data

A catalogue record for this publication is available from the British Library.

Author: Sally Morgan
Illustrator: Ángeles Peinador (Beehive)
Series editor: Rebecca Adlard
Commissioning editor: Zoë Clarke
Publishing manager: Lisa Todd
Product managers: Jennifer Hall and Caroline Green
In-house editor: Alma Puts Keren
Project manager: Emily Hooton
Editor: Matthew Hancock
Proofreaders: Natalie Murray and Michael Lamb
Cover designer: Kevin Robbins
Typesetter: 2Hoots Publishing Services Ltd
Audio produced by id audio, London
Reading guide author: Emma Wilkinson
Production controller: Rachel Weaver
Printed and bound by: GPS Group, Slovenia

Download the audio for this book and a reading guide for parents and teachers at www.collins.co.uk/839680